Little Mole Goes to School

by Glenys Nellist
illustrated by Sally Garland

beaming books
MINNEAPOLIS

For Gareth, in memory of us singing as we walked to school. I love you, Mum. —G.N.

For Johnny. —S.G.

Text copyright © 2022 Glenys Nellist

Illustrations by Sally Garland, copyright © 2022 Beaming Books

Published in 2022 by Beaming Books, an imprint of 1517 Media. All rights reserved.
No part of this book may be reproduced without the written permission of the publisher.
Email copyright@1517.media. Printed in Canada.

28 27 26 25 24 23 22   1 2 3 4 5 6 7 8

Hardcover ISBN: 978-1-5064-7859-3
eBook ISBN: 978-1-5064-8351-1

Library of Congress Cataloging-in-Publication Data

Names: Nellist, Glenys, 1959- author. | Garland, Sally Anne, illustrator.
Title: Little Mole goes to school / by Glenys Nellist ; illustrated by
   Sally Garland.
Description: Minneapolis, MN : Beaming Books, 2022. | Series: Little Mole |
   Audience: Ages 3-8. | Summary: It is the first day at Woodland School
   and little Mole is worried because he does not have Hare's ears or
   Squirrel's sharp eyesight--but when he and his friends are trapped in a
   collapsed tunnel it is little Mole who knows what to do.
Identifiers: LCCN 2021041673 (print) | LCCN 2021041674 (ebook) | ISBN
   9781506478593 (hardcover) | ISBN 9781506483511 (ebook)
Subjects: LCSH: Moles (Animals)--Juvenile fiction. | Forest
   animals--Juvenile fiction. | First day of school--Juvenile fiction. |
   Friendship--Juvenile fiction. | CYAC: Moles (Animals)--Fiction. | Forest
   animals--Fiction. | Animals--Fiction. | First day of school--Fiction. |
   Schools--Fiction. | Friendship--Fiction. | LCGFT: Picture books.
Classification: LCC PZ7.1.N433 Liw 2022 (print) | LCC PZ7.1.N433 (ebook)
   | DDC [E]--dc23
LC record available at https://lccn.loc.gov/2021041673
LC ebook record available at https://lccn.loc.gov/2021041674

VN0004589; 9781506478593; MAY2022

Beaming Books
PO Box 1209
Minneapolis, MN 55440-1209

Beamingbooks.com

It was Little Mole's first day of school.
But Little Mole was worried.

"Little Mole, whatever is wrong?" asked Mama
as they made their way along the winding path
that led to Woodland School.

"Oh, Mama," said Little Mole, "I don't think
I want to go to school. I don't know my alphabet.
And what if I can't see and hear the teacher very well?
You know that we moles don't have good eyesight,
and we're not very good at hearing, either."

"Oh, Little Mole," said Mama kindly, "lots of your friends won't know their alphabet. That's why everyone goes to school—to learn. And it will help a little if you sit near the front. I know you'll do your best, like you always do!"

At the school gate, Mama gave Little Mole a big hug and blew him a kiss goodbye as he slowly shuffled inside.

"Good morning, Little Mole!" Mrs. Badger said with a smile. "Welcome to Woodland School!"

Little Mole slid into a seat and looked around. The classroom was bright and cheery. Little Mole smiled nervously at his friends.

There, in the back row, was Little Hare. His ears were huge! He was so good at hearing.

I wish I had ears like that, thought Little Mole.

Sitting next to Little Hare was Little Squirrel, who had amazing eyesight. She was so good at seeing things.

I wish I had eyes like that, thought Little Mole.

And right in the middle, already singing the ABCs in a lovely voice, was Little Lark. She was so good at singing.

I wish I could sing the alphabet like that,
thought Little Mole.

All morning, Little Mole had to strain his little ears to hear what his teacher said.

And all morning, he had to squint carefully to see the alphabet chart. Little Mole tried his best, but he was so glad when it was time for recess.

All the animals headed out onto the playground. Little Mole was about to start swinging when he saw Little Squirrel running in circles near the base of a big old tree.

"Check this out!" Little Squirrel called excitedly. "I found a secret tunnel!" Little Mole, Little Hare, and Little Lark hurried over and peered inside the dark tunnel.

"Shall we see where it goes?" Little Hare asked. All the friends nodded and tiptoed inside.

"Wow!" said Little Mole. "This is awesome! I wonder who lived here."

But just as they were about to leave, the tunnel behind them collapsed. The four friends were trapped!

"We need help!" cried Little Hare.

"I can't dig!" cried Little Lark.

"It's so dark!" cried Little Squirrel.

But Little Mole had no problem
seeing in the dark. And he could
dig! He looked at his paws—
they were as big as shovels.

"Don't be afraid!" he said as Little Lark began to cry.
"I'll have us all out of here in no time. Follow me!"

Little Mole dug furiously to make a new tunnel.

Little Squirrel used her sharp eyes to look for signs of daylight.

Little Hare used his big ears to listen for the sounds
of the playground.

And Little Lark stopped crying and used her lovely voice to teach her friends the alphabet song to help keep them calm.

In no time at all, the four friends clambered out of the tunnel.

"Little Mole," said Little Lark, "thank you so much for rescuing us! You are so good at digging!"

Little Mole beamed. "Thanks," he said shyly. "We all used what we're good at to help each other!"

When school was over,
Little Mole rushed out
and gave his mama a huge hug.
"Mama, I love school!" he said excitedly.

"I'm learning my alphabet, I made some new friends,
and guess what? We're all good at different things!"

Mama smiled. "Oh, Little Mole, I'm so glad you had a good day."

Paw in paw, Mama and Little Mole sang and skipped all the way home.

He couldn't wait to go back to school tomorrow.

Did You Know?

MOLES

- Moles have curved front paws that dig like shovels.

- They can dig 18 feet (about the length of a pickup truck) in one hour.

- Their favorite food is worms, but they also like ants and spiders.

HARES

- Hares have big ears that swivel around in all directions to listen for danger.

- Unlike rabbits, hares do not burrow. They live above the ground.

- In danger, hares run in a zigzag pattern, sometimes as fast as 40 miles per hour! (That's the speed a car often goes!)

LARKS

- Larks are small birds that sing while they fly. Their songs can last for up to an hour!

- Larks build their nests on the ground. Their eggs are gray with brown spots.

- Larks eat seeds, slugs, grasshoppers, caterpillars, and spiders.

SQUIRRELS

- Squirrels have very good eyesight. They can see what is above or next to them without moving their heads.

- Sometimes, a squirrel rubs its face on an acorn before burying it. This covers the acorn with the squirrel's scent, and he can use his sense of smell to find it!

- In danger, squirrels make a loud chirping noise and flick their tails over their heads.

Helping a Child Who Is Anxious About Starting School

by Andrew Gladstone-Highland, LMSW
Child and Family Therapist

1. Keep in mind that any change or transition is stressful, even when it is a mostly positive change. Tell your child that it is okay to have mixed feelings about this change, to feel more than one thing at the same time.

2. See what practical things you can do that will give your child more information about what school will be like. Contact the teacher, talk with friends, practice walking to school, or get everything ready for their first day. Taking practical steps to prepare may help your child feel more control over an intimidating situation. Additionally, think about what you can do to celebrate at the end of the first day. You could start a countdown calendar to mark off the days until this celebration, to reframe anxiety about the school day.

3. Talk about times when your child has done hard things before—starting preschool, making new friends, trying a new activity, or playing on a new team. Remembering their past successes may help children feel more confident that they can take on this new challenge. You can also talk about times when you, as caregivers, have had to do new things, either as children or as adults. This will help normalize all the feelings that your child may be having around new experiences.

4. If your child seems to be overly negative, pessimistic, or fearful about the new school year, then gently point out that it is normal to have these thoughts and feelings under stress, but that we should try to challenge thoughts and feelings that seem irrational, such as: "No one will like me," "Everyone is going to be smarter than me," "My teacher is going to be mean," or "I'll never like going to school." Emphasize with your child that you will deal, together, with whatever challenges come.

5. Practice calming coping strategies, such as deep breathing, regular mealtimes and bedtimes, and exercise. Do things that you enjoy doing together—drawing, reading, playing outside, going for walks.

GLENYS NELLIST is the author of multiple children's books, including *Little Mole Finds Hope*, the bestselling *'Twas the Evening of Christmas*, and the popular series Love Letters from God and Snuggle Time. Her writing reflects a deep passion for helping children discover joy in the world. Glenys lives in Michigan with her husband, David.

SALLY GARLAND was brought up in the small town of Alness in the Highlands of Scotland and studied illustration at Edinburgh College of Art. She currently lives and works in Glasgow, with her partner and young son. Garland has loved drawing and has had a passion for children's literature and illustration since she was young. She now has many years of experience working as a children's illustrator. Her current influences include vintage picture book illustration from the 1950s and 1960s.